爆 BAKUGAN™
BATTLE BRAWLERS

HOW TO DRAW

Written and Illustrated by Ron Zalme

ISBN-13: 978- 0-545-12099-9   ISBN-10: 0-545-12099-3

12 11 10 9 8 7 6 5 4 3 2 1   9 10 11 12/0

Interior designed by Rocco Melillo
Printed in the U.S.A.
First printing, January 2009

SCHOLASTIC INC.

New York   Toronto   London   Auckland   Sydney
Mexico City   New Delhi   Hong Kong   Buenos Aires

PREPARE TO DRAW

The cards are placed and the Bakugan stand! BATTLE BRAWL! Ever wonder what the close-up action of a battle between Bakugan titans would really be like? Now you can go beyond the excitement of the game and the show and find out. How? With a simple pencil and eraser! Follow the steps as outlined in this guide and you'll be drawing all your favorite Bakugan characters in no time. Design, sketch, and detail from the provided poses and you'll learn all the shapes and lines necessary to render the brawlers and their Bakugan guardian. Develop your skills and you'll evolve to be a true Bakugan master artist!

DAN

As leader of the brawlers, Dan's life revolves around playing Bakugan. He's a master of the power play and using fire attributes in battle!

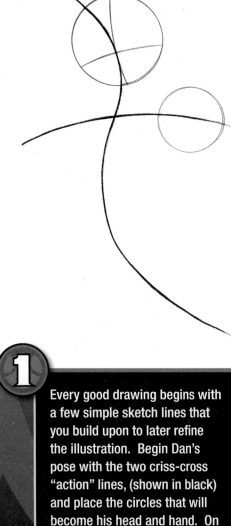

1 Every good drawing begins with a few simple sketch lines that you build upon to later refine the illustration. Begin Dan's pose with the two criss-cross "action" lines, (shown in black) and place the circles that will become his head and hand. On the larger head circle, add the "crosshairs"; the vertical and horizontal lines that will help you place the facial features later.

2 Around the action lines, begin to construct Dan's body with cubes and cylinders, the kind of shapes that add volume! Follow the new blue lines to build on your sketch.

3 Time to start adding in the details! Follow the illustration to draw in Dan's glasses, hair, vest, belt . . . and his Bakugan sphere, too!

4 Notice how the details are "fitted" over your initial sketch? That's the secret to drawing! Start simple with large easy shapes and build your figure with more and more detail.

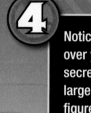

5 Almost done! Erase your early sketch lines and reinforce the lines that best describe your character with darker pencil, or even a marker. Don't expect perfection with your first try. Being an artist takes practice . . . just like rolling a Bakugan ball onto a Gateway card!

DRAGO

Pyrus Drago is Dan's guardian and friend. He's the leader of all the Bakugan and also one of the most powerful. Using his intense heat attribute, he can dissolve all that surrounds him in battle!

1

Once again, start with the action lines to capture the basic pose of the character. Overlap the circles and ovals as shown in blue to begin building a "framework" upon which to construct Drago.

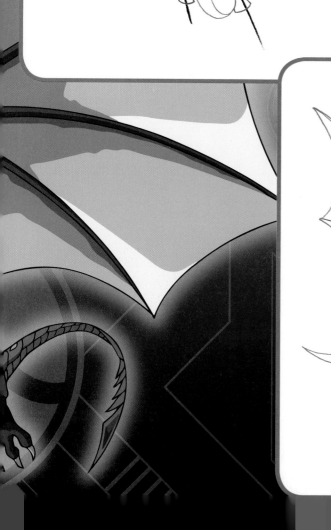

2

Sketch in the large bat-like wings and then rough in the additional shapes needed to form the body. Now's a good time to sketch in the blade-like horn on his nose, too!

3

Now draw the "ribs" that support the skin of Drago's huge wings and then add in some of his facial details. You can also add his feet and tail.

4

Drago is a complex character, so pay close attention to adding the extra horns and muscle shapes.

5

Continue filling in the details that give Drago his fearsome dragonoid form. Pay particular attention to the lines that add detail to his combat nose horn!

 6

The main task in this step is to add the ribbing that constructs the defensive scales of Drago's underbelly. Note how they're really a set of "V" shapes built along the lines you drew earlier.

 **7**

Okay . . . time to clean up your drawing! Erase the lines you no longer need and emphasize the ones that clearly depict Drago. Finish your drawing in ink or marker and add color, too!

Did you know that as one of the most powerful species living in Vestroia, Pyrus Drago is able to infinitely evolve on his own? Plus, as a Pyrus-based dragonoid knight, he has the ability to blitz his enemies from every angle like a raging firestorm!

SHUN

Shun approaches the strategy of playing Bakugan with the cunning of a Ninja warrior. His battle technique hinges on his ability to wield the wind!

1 Begin with the usual flowing action lines and proceed to place the large oval for Shun's head. Add in the shapes required to construct the body as well.

2 Now start adding the "building blocks" to fill out the body shape; rectangles, circles, cylinders. Try to capture the motion of Shun's athletic form.

3 Use the previous step's shapes as a framework to add Shun's clothing details and flowing hair. Don't worry if the lines aren't exact . . . they'll look better loose and graceful than forced and confined.

4 Carefully draw in the final details of Shun's features and costume. Keep your sketching light until you're certain where you want to put your line!

5 Clean up your drawing and eliminate all unnecessary lines. Remember to keep the fluidity of the pose alive by not overworking the lines. Keep it light until you've got it right!

SKYRESS

Ventus Skyress is a bird-beast life-form and Shun's personal Bakugan. She is clairvoyant, meaning that she has the power to see objects and events that cannot be perceived by normal senses. Her attribute in battle is the use of gale-force wind!

1

Start with the large "U" shape to define the spread of the wings. Be sure to keep the small sketched circles for the head and body in proportion, or your final drawing will have very small wings.

2 Define the outline for all the wing feathers with a broad shape as shown . . . save the detail for later! Add in the shapes for the feet and the double spikes that rise from the top of her head.

3 Sketch in the additional lines to define the shapes of the three tiers of feathers that you'll be adding soon. Also add detail to the feet . . . and to make things less confusing, let's just draw only a couple of her tail feathers at this stage.

4 Don't worry about exactly drawing every feather or the number of feathers. If you get close, the final result will be just as effective.

5 Okay, now do the second row of wing feathers, and add some more detail to the tail feathers as well.

6

Draw the final row of feathers and add the intricate detail to the wing interiors. Any complex drawing can be simplified by approaching it this way! Group the details into a single shape . . . and then refine each portion individually.

Being of the Skyress species, this Bakugan can not only evolve . . . she has the ultimate ability to resurrect herself, too! And if her gigantic wingspan and sharp-tipped tail feathers aren't enough to contend with in battle, she has the speed and power of a hurricane at her command!

7

Time to erase and clean up your drawing! With all that detail, does your drawing look "smudgy"? If so, consider using a harder pencil to draw with . . . like a 3H or 5H lead. Your local art supply store should have them.

RUNO

Runo isn't your typical pre-teen girl! She's a tomboy to the extreme . . . and though she's only twelve, she can brawl with the best of them in her favorite game . . . Bakugan!

1 Runo's action lines need to be very "fluid" to capture her graceful pose; notice how the vertical line resembles a smooth backwards "S." Place the circle for the head just above the action line for the shoulders and add the "crosshairs" to later align the features. Block in the body shapes as shown. Her flowing pigtails can be represented by two simple lines.

2 Draw the shape of Runo's face within the circle drawn in step one, and place her eyes along the horizontal crosshair. Continue by framing up the remaining limbs; arms, calves, and feet. Simplify the shapes of difficult body parts, like hands, by refining them to their basics . . . circles, rectangles, etc.

3 Now that most of the figure is roughed in, you can begin adding detail. Draw in the ruffles for the skirt and blouse . . . and draw the locks of hair that define her bangs. Notice the additional detail for the eyes that can be added in this step!

4 All the extra frills of hair and costume details can now be fitted over your initial sketch. Just as real clothes would be fitted over a mannequin, your drawn clothing needs to be fitted over your sketched framework!

5 Almost done! Erase your beginning sketch lines and darken the lines that best define Runo's figure and costume! Have fun with the hair too. . . . Don't feel confined by the example, be stylish!

TIGRERRA

Haos Tigrerra is Runo's personal Bakugan. Within her body she conceals a mighty blade capable of slicing through anything in the known human world! And if that's not enough . . . Tigrerra can also evolve!

1

Begin with your action lines set like an "X," but with long, curved strokes. The large circle for the body is set just off-center of the "X" and the structure for the head can be drawn within it as shown. Simple is always the best way to start, so sketch in simple shapes that will later become an arm and a leg.

2 Starting at the shoulder, sketch in each of the shapes that will define Tigrerra's left arm. Add in three spikes along her back at this time and sketch in the clusters of "egg" shapes that will become her fingers and toes. Don't forget her tail!

3 The shapes of the face need to be distinct, so carefully add in the features and daggerlike fins that extend from her cheeks. Construct more of her arms and legs as shown and use the "egg clusters" to position and sketch the ferocious claws!

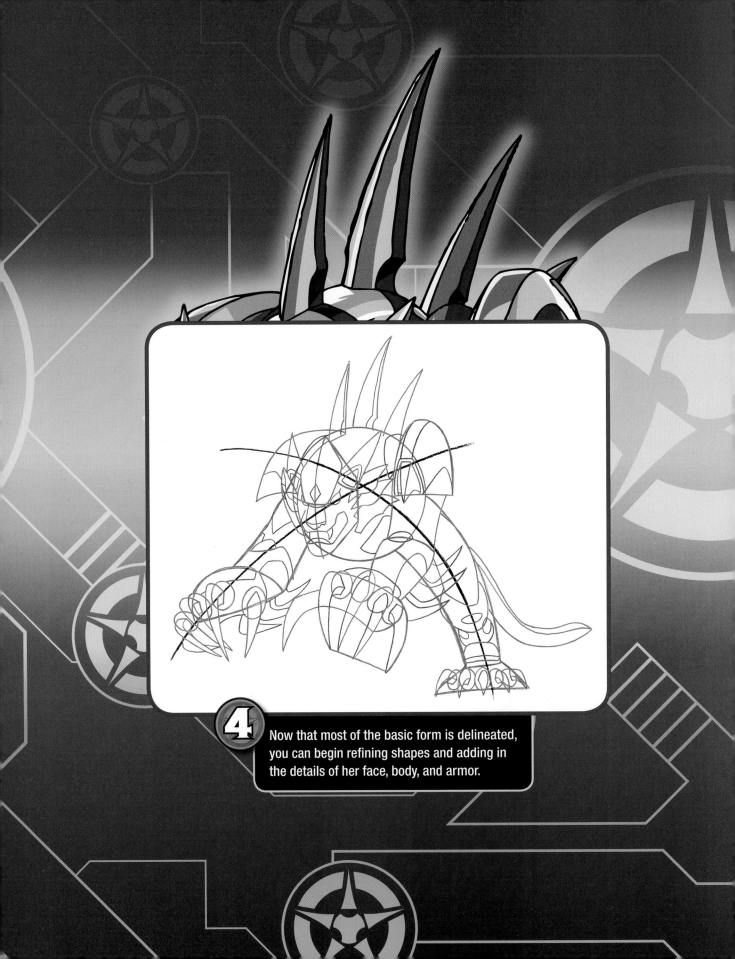

4 Now that most of the basic form is delineated, you can begin refining shapes and adding in the details of her face, body, and armor.

5

Most of the figure is already described now, but Tigrerra still needs a right foot in back! Sketch in the basic circles between her left arm and leg to construct it in a dynamic running pose. The rest of the work in this step is adding armor details and costume designs.

6 Complete Tigrerra's right foot and continue drawing in the details of her body armor.

Tigrerra has the mythical ability to control and manipulate light and energy, drawing her power from the planet Haos. Haos is a planet with a mystical aura so bright that it leaves a lasting "flashbulb" effect on even the most protected eyes!

7 Time to clean up your drawing! There's lots of detail, so be careful when erasing! Sometimes it helps to use just the edge of your eraser to clean up between thin lines!

MARUCHO

Like a walking encyclopedia, Marucho uses data and analysis to form his Bakugan strategies. But if that's not enough, he's got the power of water to back him up in battle!

1 Now that you're getting the hang of it, let's try adding a few more shapes into the first step. Start with the action lines, draw the large circle for the head and fit in the other shapes to construct Marucho's body.

2 Add the basic features and hair, then start to sketch in the form of the clothing. Keep it light and loose!

3 Add more detail to the eyes and draw in the glasses. Also add some of the clothing details now. Note the addition of Marucho's right arm behind his body. This helps to give "depth" to the figure.

4 Now it's time for the small stuff. You should have a sturdy framework to add in all the folds and wrinkles, fingernails, and stray hair.

5 Now you can erase and clean up your drawing! Would you like a tip to avoid erasing? Put a clean sheet of paper over your sketch and use any nearby window as a light source to trace your drawing fresh!

PREYAS

Aquos Preyas, Marucho's guardian, is like a chameleon . . . he has the ability to mimic all of the Bakugan attributes: fire, earth, light, darkness, water, and wind!

1 Center your action guidelines and then place the circles and ovals along it as shown. The single blue lines are used here as action lines, too.

2

Work in large shapes. Construct Preyas' heavily muscled body as shown and use the crosshairs on the face to place his features. Also draw the basic shape of his frill—the fan shape behind his head.

3

Start to form the hands and feet and add in the bat-like wings that attach to his forearms. Draw the ribs that support the frill.

4

Preyas has lots of body detail, so let's start blocking some of it in now. Define the edge of the frill, add fingers and toes, and add the arm-wing ribs.

5

Okay, your drawing is starting to look a lot like Preyas . . . but it's a little stiff looking, right? In this step we'll change the basic shapes of his body into the more "natural-looking" shapes of bone and muscle. Follow the diagram and alter the arms and legs to look more like super strong limbs!

6 Now that Preyas looks more lifelike, let's add all the fine body details: scales, webbing, and spikes. Take your time and work on one section at a time.

7 Clean up the drawing and rework some of your lines if you need to. Cross check your artwork with the character art provided. Did you work in all the details? Spectacular!

The peculiar structure of the nuclei in Preyas' molecules gives him the unique ability to display the characteristics of all the other attributes at will! Also, as an Aquos Bakugan, he can seamlessly glide from one attack position to the next—a very deadly maneuver!

JULIE

Don't let Julie fool you! First impressions might sway you to think she was just bubbly and a bit clueless . . . but she's a master of direct attacks and uses earth attributes when battle brawling! With Gorem at her side, you might want to rethink those "first impressions" . . .

1 Because of the wide stance of the character, it's wise to add an additional action line here . . . one that defines the hips. Draw the short horizontal line first and then add the longer lines of the legs radiating from it. Now draw the head and appendage framework.

2 Continue to rough in the body foundation and also add in the eyes and face structure.

More detail can be added to the facial features now, particularly the eyes. Notice the open circle over the darker pupil . . . a clever trick used in the anime style of drawing to simulate a highlight reflecting from the eye. Continue on by adding the costume details.

Now that all the larger shapes and details have been sketched in, you can focus on the even smaller details; belt rivets, hair wisps . . . and of course, Julie's Bakugan card and ball!

Julie's done! You just have to erase away your unwanted sketch lines. Notice how her shorts and boot cuffs seem to wrap around her legs, not just across them. Details like that give the drawing its dynamic 3-D look!

GOREM

Subterra Gorem is Julie's earth-attribute Bakugan. His entire body is composed of extremely hard and dense cell-bodies . . . making him exceptionally solid and heavy! Like Drago, Subterra Gorem has the ability to evolve!

1

Sketch the two action lines as shown and then begin to align the six spheres you will need to define the body. The central shape of the torso is a bit difficult, but compare your sketch to each quadrant formed by the action lines to get it right.

2 Draw in the structural shapes to define the body and limbs. Use the shapes you created in step one as "anchors" from which to extend these new shapes. Pay close attention to the finger shapes that form a fist in the upper left corner.

3 Now that the "flat" framework has been sketched in, this new series of lines and shapes in this step will help to give your drawing "volume" . . . a 3-D appearance. Start simple and build up!

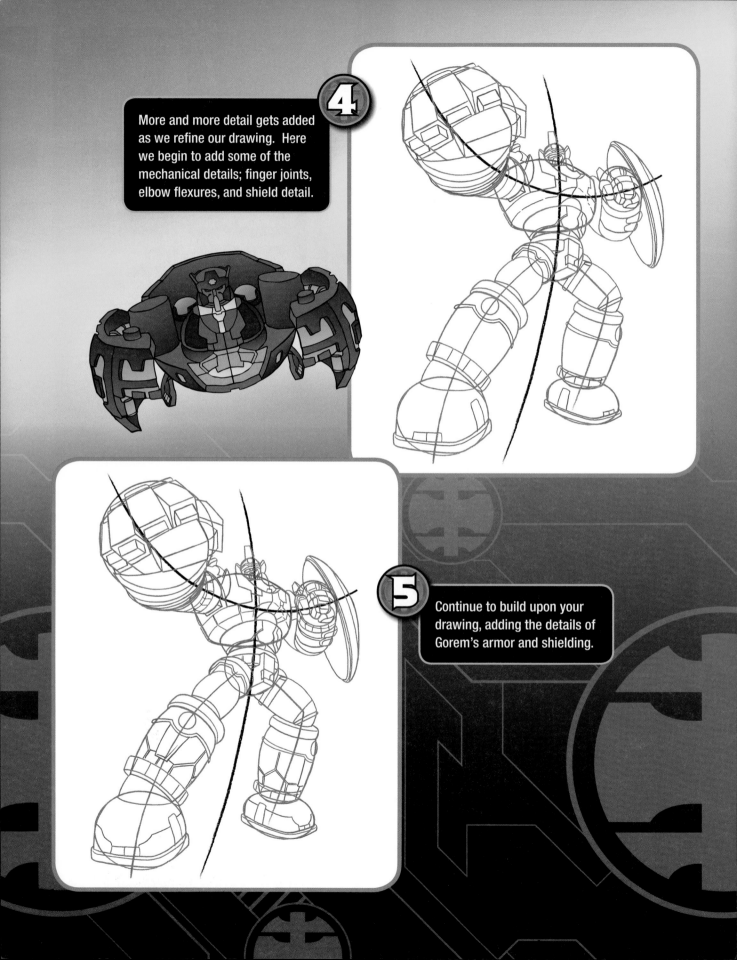

4

More and more detail gets added as we refine our drawing. Here we begin to add some of the mechanical details; finger joints, elbow flexures, and shield detail.

5

Continue to build upon your drawing, adding the details of Gorem's armor and shielding.

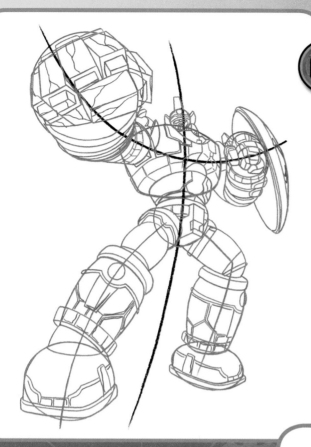

 The purpose of this step is primarily to add the "organic" elements of Gorem's figure. He's an earth-attribute Bakugan, so he needs cracks and stone texturing to make him look . . . well, "earthy"!

7 Erase and embolden your linework for a truly imposing figure of Gorem! Want a challenge? Try drawing a "mirror" image of this or any of your other favorite poses! Just flip the pose. Sound easy? Try it! (Hint: use a real mirror . . . it helps!)

Gorem is a product of the harsh and brutal landscape of the rugged world known as Subterra. Subterrans are at ease both above and below ground and their battle style reflects the raw power of earth and stone in cataclysmic upheaval. In anger, Gorem is like an earthquake unleashed. Luckily, Julie has the ability to calm him!

MASQUERADE

Masquerade was a master of the darkness attribute, but more disturbing, was that no one knew who he really was . . . AND he held the DOOM card, a card that could suddenly banish any Bakugan to the Doom Dimension!

1 Sketch your action lines and then locate and place the head circle. From there you can situate the other basic body elements along the axis of the action lines.

2 Draw the hair in sections to avoid having to manage such a complex shape all at once.

Continue extending Masquerade's arms and legs, and rough in some of the fabric shapes of his clothing . . . keep it loose and flowing!

4

Now you can add in the rest of the hair shapes and begin to focus on details such as fingers, armbands, and belt buckles.

5

In this step, all the final detail gets added! Compare your drawing closely to the diagram and see if you've captured all of Masquerade's mysteriousness!

HYDRANOID

Darkus Hydranoid was Masquerade's devoted Bakugan and now belongs to Alice. When in battle, he might be a bit slower than other Bakugan . . . but he makes up for it by being cruel and merciless!

1

Begin with the action lines almost forming two "U" shapes facing up and down. Place a large circle at the center of the drawing . . . this will help to define the chest area of Hydranoid. Sketch in the rest of the shapes as shown.

2 Connect your basic shapes with long curving tubes to give Hydranoid's body a "snake-like" appearance. Then extend the front and rear legs from the sides of the tube to give him a solid stance.

3 Hydranoid's scales and spikes are one of his best defensive weapons . . . start to add them in this step! Note how the lower jaw, tongue, and horns are fitted to the head circle.

4

Sketch in the vicious rows of teeth and continue adding more spikes to the head and body. Add more armor plating around the legs and feet, too!

Darkus Bakugan are grandmasters of night-fighting and thrive in shadow. They gain power from the dark and concentrate it to cause tremendous destruction!

5

Follow the curves of Hydranoid's body and add armor plating from his head to his tail. Keep the lines curved so that they appear to go around the shape of his body. Straight lines will make your drawing appear flat.

6

Complete the detail for the head and draw in the rows of osteoderms, the bony armor ridges common to dinosaurs, crocodiles . . . and Hydranoid dragons!

7

Clear away all your unwanted sketch lines and refine the lines that best show off Hydranoid's fearsome armor and offensive spikes! Did you add all the barbs to his tail?

HAL-G

Once a simple research scientist, Hal-G (previously known as Michael) was the first to discover a portal between Earth and Vestroia. However, after teleporting himself through the portal, he was engulfed by the evil forces of the Silent Core and transformed into a maniacal villain bent on destroying all the Bakugan.

1

The central vertical action line indicates the "center of gravity" of the figure . . . add the other two lines to indicate the positioning for the arms and legs. Place the head circle and then block in the body shape as well as the hand and feet.

2

Use the head circle to place the basic features and add the pointed chin. Using the action lines as a guide, sketch in the cylindrical shapes that give the arms and legs form and structure.

3 Add detail to Hal's eyeglasses and add the wisps of hair that help give him that "mad-scientist" look. You can also add his cloak and staff at this time.

4 Now that the basic foundations are drawn, you can add in the details of Hal's clothing, club, cape, and pendant . . . right down to the veins on his forehead!

5 Clean up the drawing and eliminate all the structural sketch lines with your eraser. In fact, considering how evil Hal is . . . maybe you should erase him entirely! Just kidding . . .

ALICE

Alice is a Russian girl whose body had been possessed by Masquerade! His evil plan was to send all Bakugan to the Doom Dimension so his guardian, Hydranoid, would be the strongest. When he was ultimately defeated by Dan, Alice was once again returned to her true self.

1

Sketch in the action lines and add the head circle. Work down from there and it should help you to place the basic shapes for Alice's figure.

2

Lightly sketch in the flowing shapes of hair and clothing . . . and draw the arms and legs along the previously drawn action lines.

Carefully render the facial features and add more wisps of flowing hair. The hands and feet can be developed further at this point as well.

4

Time to add in all the final details . . . refine her features, add more hair, soften the lines of her body, and render the fashion details of her outfit!

5

Eraser time! Get rid of the unnecessary construction lines and concentrate on the line work that describes the figure best. Hint: Keep the line work soft.

CONGRATULATIONS!

You've completed all the exercises and evolved to master Bakugan artist!
Now that you have the basics, try drawing your favorite characters in
different poses! Then draw them battling each other for the
ultimate Bakugan championship! Brawlers take aim . . . !